We found a
SEED

A book to share from
Scallywag Press

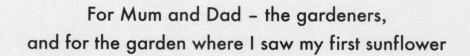

For Mum and Dad – the gardeners,
and for the garden where I saw my first sunflower

First published in Great Britain in 2019
by Scallywag Press Ltd, 10 Sutherland Row, London SW1V 4JT

Printed on FSC paper in China by Toppan Leefung

001

British Library Cataloguing in Publication Data available
ISBN 978-1-912650-08-8

ROB RAMSDEN

We found a SEED

Scallywag Press Ltd

LONDON

This is us.

We found a seed!

We put it in a box
to keep it safe.

It didn't grow.

We played with the seed.

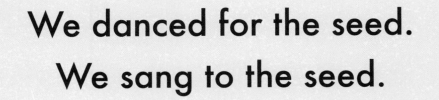

We danced for the seed.
We sang to the seed.

It didn't grow.

We asked the seed,
"What must we do?"

We listened,

we waited,

and then we heard . . .

"Plant me."

And so we did!

We dug a small bed
and tucked the seed in.

We heard the wind
blow autumn leaves.

Did the seed hear it too?

We felt the icy
winter rain.

Did the seed feel it too?

We were warmed by the sun
in early spring.

The seed was too.

It grew . . .

and it grew,

and it grew . . .

and it grew.

It gave us a flower!

It shone like the sun
all summer long.

Then autumn came.

Our flower died
and we were sad.

But it left us
a gift . . .

It gave us seeds!

We knew just what to do.